THE
HUMMINGBIRD KING

To my husband, Samuel Zeigler,
critic, helper, friend.

Library of Congress Cataloging-in-Publication Data

Palacios, Argentina.
   The hummingbird king: a Guatemalan legend / written and adapted
by Argentina Palacios; illustrated by Felipe Davalos.
      p.   cm.—(Legends of the world)
   Summary: A young chief who had been protected by a hummingbird is
killed by his jealous uncle and then transformed into a quetzal,
symbol of freedom.
   ISBN 0-8167-3051-2 (lib. bdg.)   ISBN 0-8167-3052-0 (pbk.)
   1. Mayas—Legends.   2. Quetzals—Folklore.   [1. Mayas—Legends.
2. Indians of Central America—Guatemala—Legends.   3. Folklore—
Guatemala.]   I. Davalos, Felipe, ill.   II. Title.   III. Series.
F1465.P36   1993
398.2´097281—dc20   92-21437

LEGENDS OF THE WORLD

THE HUMMINGBIRD KING

A GUATEMALAN LEGEND

WRITTEN AND ADAPTED BY ARGENTINA PALACIOS
ILLUSTRATED BY FELIPE DAVALOS

TROLL ASSOCIATES

 YRAMIDS, PALACES, and temples of stone stand silent and abandoned, hidden by dense rain forests. But that was not always so. Long, long ago, great cities built by the Mayan people were centers of activity.

In one of those cities — one whose name has long been forgotten — there lived an old *halac uinic,* or chief. Since he had no son to succeed him, he knew that his younger brother, Chirumá, would one day take his place.

But the chief's wife wanted a child. Each day, she prayed with all her heart. And, one day, her prayers were answered. She gave birth to a son. The child was born on the 13th day of the month, a lucky day. For the number 13 reminded the Mayan people of their 13 heavens.

Just as the baby was being born, another sign appeared. A beautiful hummingbird perched on a tree branch in front of the stately residence. It was not an ordinary bird, but the largest and most brightly colored hummingbird anyone had ever seen. No one had ever remembered a bird of its kind standing still for so long.

The high priest determined that this was an omen. "The messenger of the gods has come," he said. "He is telling us that this child will be extraordinary, just like this hummingbird."

In the days that followed, a special naming ceremony took place. The high priest gave the chief and his wife a bright red feather he'd found beneath the tree branch where the hummingbird perched.

"We shall name our son Kukul," the chief's wife proclaimed. "That name means 'beautiful feather.'"

"And so shall this feather protect the boy as long as he carries it with him," the priest said.

A great celebration took place in the public plaza. Everyone joined the festivities. Everyone was happy, except Chirumá. He knew that, because of this child, he would never become *halac uinic*.

10

UKUL GREW INTO a handsome young man with jet black hair and skin the color of cinnamon. He was quick of mind and excelled at any task he was given. As a young boy, he spent long hours with his father. Together, they would study the stars.

Like all Mayan boys, Kukul learned the art of warfare from his elders. He made his own spears, bows, and arrows — straight and strong as the boy himself.

Soon the time came for Kukul to take his place among the men of his nation. A nomad tribe was attempting a raid. Kukul, Chirumá, and the others went to war. Showers of spears and arrows rained down. Kukul fought bravely, at times at the very front. But wherever he was, not a single weapon fell on him.

Chirumá observed this. "The gods must watch out for Kukul," he thought to himself.

All at once, Kukul saw an arrow flying straight toward Chirumá, and Kukul positioned himself like a shield in front of his uncle. The arrow changed its course and fell to the ground without harming anyone. The enemy fled in astonishment and Kukul turned toward the wounded.

"How could it be that Kukul never gets hurt?" Chirumá wondered. "He must have a strong charm. I will find out."

That night, as Kukul slept on his straw mat, Chirumá came upon him. He carefully searched Kukul's sleeping body, but found nothing. Then he saw it — a large red feather barely sticking out of the straw mat.

"His charm!" Chirumá said cheerfully to himself, as he carefully lifted the feather from its hiding place.

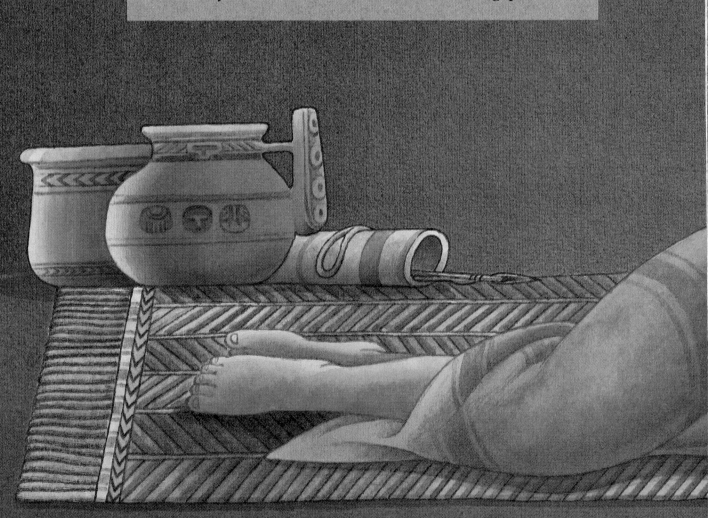

When Kukul awoke, he saw that the feather was gone. He searched everywhere, but he could not find it. Nor could he remember the words of the priest on the day he was born. Without realizing it, Kukul had lost the charm and all the protection it provided.

It came to pass that the old chief went to the afterlife. Upon his death, all the high priests prepared to meet in council to choose a new chief. Chirumá knew that the priests would favor his nephew. He looked for the youngest priest, the one he knew could be easily swayed.

"Kukul is not a hero," he said. "Arrows never fall where he places himself. He is afraid to fight."

"No, he is not," said the priest. "Kukul is using his intelligence to win."

Chirumá would find any opportunity to talk to that priest about Kukul. Another day, he told him, "Kukul is reckless. He stops to take care of the wounded and puts his men in danger."

"Kukul is compassionate," replied the priest.

"He is inexperienced," countered Chirumá, as he sowed the seeds of doubt.

Now according to custom, a new *halac uinic* could be anyone in the departed chief's family. The high priests met.

"It should be Kukul, without a doubt," said the oldest priest.

"It should be Kukul," the second priest chimed in.

"Yes, without a doubt," the third priest added.

There was silence. "It should be Chirumá," said the youngest. "Kukul is too young and inexperienced."

They argued about the merits of each man. In the end, no one changed his vote and Kukul was chosen as *halac uinic.*

Under his rule, there was peace throughout the land. In time, even Chirumá's friend came to appreciate that Kukul had been a good choice.

Kukul spent much time studying the stars. He made mathematical calculations. He could tell the farmers the best times to plant to reap the richest crops. Everybody was happy with Kukul, except Chirumá.

One day, Kukul was hunting in the forest. He heard the rustling of leaves and raised his bow and arrow. With a flurry, a magnificent hummingbird, larger than any hummingbird Kukul had ever seen, fluttered next to him. The hummingbird spoke these words, "I am your guardian, Kukul. My job is to warn you. Beware. Death is circling you. Beware of a man."

"Magnificent hummingbird, my guardian, what man should I beware of?" asked Kukul.

"Someone very close to you. Be careful, Kukul," said the bird. Then it flew away.

Kukul walked on through the forest. As he came to a thicket, he heard the faint rustling of leaves. He pointed his arrow, but saw nothing. Kukul crouched low to the ground and moved slowly. He had not gone far when . . . sssss . . . it came. An arrow pierced his chest.

In pain, Kukul pulled out the arrow and headed for the river to wash his wound. "Surely, it is not deep," he tried to convince himself, but his strength began to fade as his chest turned scarlet with blood.

A few more steps and Kukul had to lean against a tree. "It is so dark," he moaned. He fell onto a sea of emerald grass and there he died. Alone. Betrayed.

Then, something extraordinary happened. Slowly, Kukul's body changed to the color of the grass, but his chest remained scarlet. His skin became feathers and his hair, a gorgeous crest.

By the time Chirumá came out of the thicket, Kukul's arms had turned into wings. All Chirumá could see was a glowing green bird with a scarlet chest and a long, long tail, flying off into the sunlight.

The people mourned the loss of Kukul, but after a time, Chirumá was chosen to be the new chief. Chirumá was a cruel and warlike king and soon after, enemies again attacked the city and in fierce battle took Chirumá prisoner. Everybody watched while his body was painted black and white, the colors of a slave. He was taken away from the city, never to be seen again.

Today, a most beautiful green bird with a scarlet chest, a long, long tail, and a gorgeous crest perches high up on the trees in the deep, cool cloud forest, watching everything and listening for the rustling of leaves.

The Mayan of old called this bird *kukul*. They carved its image into stone and placed it on their temples and palaces. Today this wise and peaceful bird — a symbol of freedom to all its people — is known as the *quetzal*.

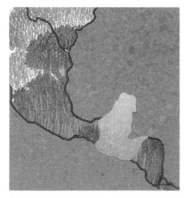

The ancient Mayas lived in present-day southern Mexico, Guatemala, Honduras, and western El Salvador. They were farmers and architects who built magnificent temples and pyramids. They were also fine artists, goldsmiths, and coppersmiths. Their social system, based on their beliefs and ideas, encouraged harmony with the environment.

The *quetzal* described in this story is found only in remote cloud forests in the highlands of Guatemala. As in *The Hummingbird King,* the bird's head and back are emerald green. There is a crest of green-and-gold feathers on its head. Its chest is scarlet. The upper tail feathers can be up to three feet (91 cm) long. In ancient times, these feathers were used to decorate ceremonial headdresses. They were a symbol of authority.

Today the *quetzal* is the national bird of Guatemala. Its image appears on postage stamps and on coins, which are also called *quetzals*.

Legends say the *quetzal* loves its freedom so much that it will die in captivity. But the cloud forests that are its natural habitat are disappearing from the earth. Happily, scientists have had some success breeding the *quetzal* in zoos and nature parks, preserving the Mayan ideal of people living in harmony with nature.

Human figure